Aunties

Printed in the United States of America
Second Printing, 2021
ISBN 978-1-7344145-3-0

Sterling, Connecticut
www.artistmarnie.com

Dedicated To…

The wonderful women and aunts in my life…
Aunt Martha, Aunt Louise, and Sandee.

In Memory of Aunt Olive, Aunt Violet, and Aunt Cil

One of my favorite things is to be called "Auntie"

To all those who consider me "Auntie", I love you.

One day, a new baby arrived in our family.

Everyone was so excited, especially me.
I finally had you!

I loved to visit you, and could
not wait to help your parents.

I helped them when they did chores.

I helped them when they were tired.

I even helped when they
just wanted to go on a date!

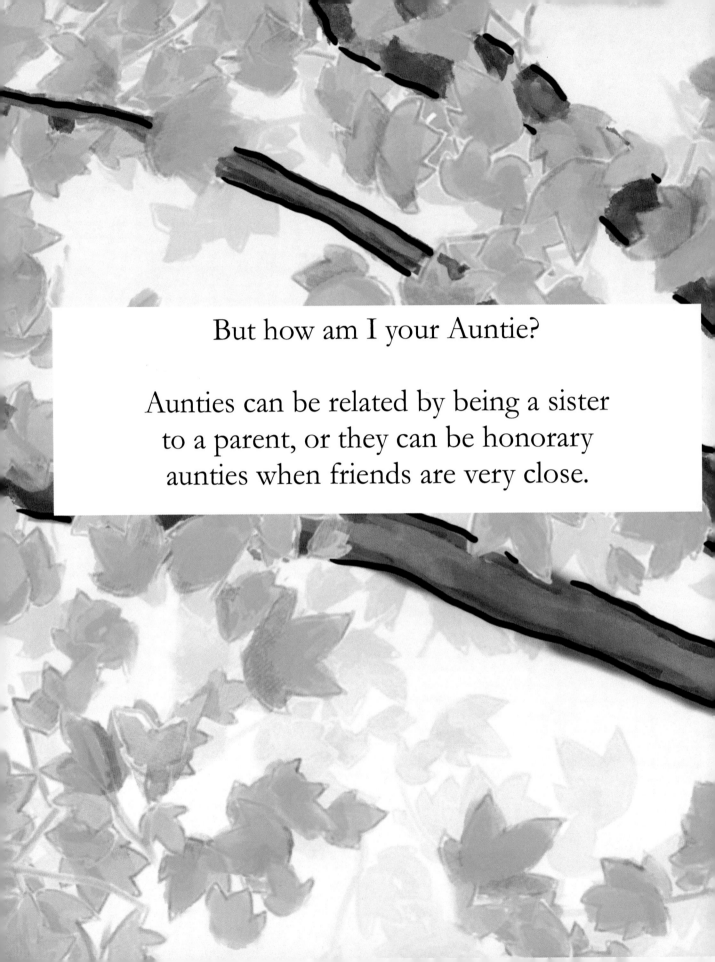

But how am I your Auntie?

Aunties can be related by being a sister
to a parent, or they can be honorary
aunties when friends are very close.

Either way, aunties are always there for you.
When you need some help…

or when you just need a hug.

Aunties can also share stories of
family members you have never met…
and even stories of your own parents!

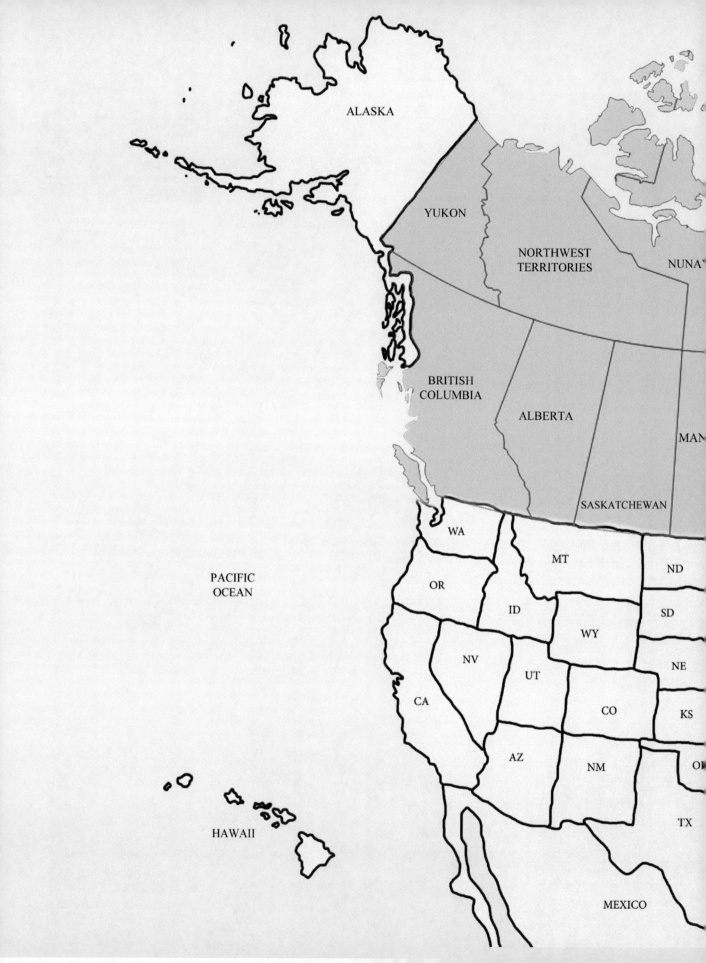

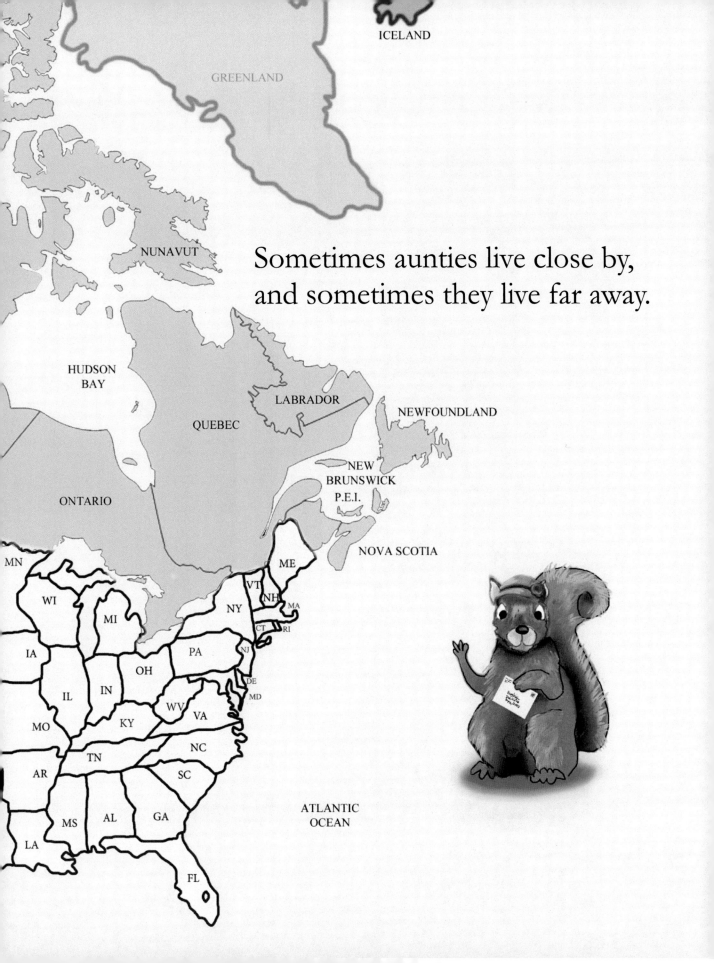

Sometimes aunties live close by,
and sometimes they live far away.

But no matter how close or far apart they are,
one thing is for sure…
an auntie's love never goes away.

One day you will grow big and strong,
and I hope you will remember our times
together and still visit with me!

Near or far. Small or big.
Always remember that I love you…

today and forever!

Ways to show an auntie you love them...

Ask your parent to
call her on the phone
to say hello!
Or text her!

Ask a parent for help
sending her a letter.

Always send her a
thank you for gifts!

Lastly always give her a big hug when you see her!
She will love it!

Thank you for reading my book!
When not writing or illustrating, I am painting and
dreaming of traveling with my loved ones.

I have a website, artistmarnie.com,
where you can see more of my colorful, happy work.

Marnie

My other books are:

The hardest part of being a Mom is your children growing up. Luckily a new little one shows her Mimi that life does go on... quite happily.

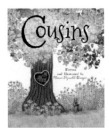

Discover where your cousins live with a map of USA and learn about family with some bushy-tailed squirrels. Then fill out a family tree together!

Read about Old Red, a children's book that shows the many things a tractor can do, and teaches an important lesson — old items can be restored and made useful.

Read all about how much Aunties love their family, and how to show you love them in return!

Read about the life of an antique car, and learn about combustion engines and the differences between modern cars and a Model A!

Join Old Red as she helps a friend at a Christmas tree farm! Enjoy festive illustrations and the joy of helping others.

Made in the USA
Las Vegas, NV
28 October 2021

33199261R00019